SUMMER WITH A BROTHER'S BEST FRIEND

LOVE BEACH COLLECTION

ALEXANDRA HALE

Copyright © 2024 by Alexandra Hale

All rights reserved.

Cover Design: Zee Irwin

Paperback Design: AK Cover Designs

Editing By: Happily Editing Anns

No part of this book may be reproduced in any form or by any electronic or mechanical means, including information storage and retrieval systems, without written permission from the author, except for the use of brief quotations in a book review.

In accordance with the Copyright Act of 1976, the scanning, uploading, and electronic sharing of any part of this book without permission of the author is unlawful piracy and theft of the author's intellectual property.

This is a work of fiction. Names, characters, businesses, places, events, and incidents are either the product of the author's imagination or used in a fictitious manner. Any resemblance to actual persons, living or dead, or actual events is purely coincidental.

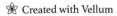 Created with Vellum

In memory of Jimmy Buffett - you will forever be the soundtrack to summer.

To Carolina - thank you for being the co-chair of chaos coordination - but seriously what have we gotten ourselves into...

1

REECE

10 WEEKS BEFORE THE END OF SUMMER

"Oh my *God,* that feels so good," I moan into the quiet space of the storeroom of Love Beach Brews. Boxes and supplies are stacked neatly on shelves against every one of the slate-gray walls, the dim lights giving off an almost romantic ambiance.

Almost.

"Shh, you're going to get us caught."

"We're not going to get caught—just... *just* like that." I moan again as I let my head fall forward.

"Your brother is going to kill me if he finds out I had my hands on you," Isaac murmurs, his breath hot against the shell of my ear.

"So, it's *my* fault my brother is your best friend?"

"No," he breathes, "it's your fault you're so damn hot and drive me fucking wild."

"Sounds like such a hardship."

"It really is."

"You could always walk away." It's an empty threat for both of us because I know without a doubt he won't—he wants this as much as I do.

He snorts, his fingers exploring as he says, "I won't do that, but you know as well as I do he's going to lose his shit when he finds out."

"Stop being so dramatic. He's not going to know," I hiss even though pleasure is coursing through my body at his touch.

"What if someone walks in?"

"No one is going to know. It's just the two of us here..."

"How can you be so sure? It's not like I locked the front door..." His words are a tease as he runs the palm of his hand up and down my spine, making me arch into his touch.

"I didn't know you were into voyeurism, Boss Man. It's kinda hot." I smirk as Isaac growls, his fingers digging into my flesh as he presses impossibly closer to me. And because I can't help myself, I add, "It's never really been my thing, but I think I can make an exception for you."

Turning my head to the side, I grin at him over my shoulder, his breath mingling with mine, his dark amber eyes absolutely blazing.

"You *know* I have no interest in sharing you."

"Do I know that?"

"I swear I'll walk away right now, Reece."

"I will smother you in your sleep if you stop." I wiggle back against him to spur him on. "I *need* you harder."

"Not sure how much harder I can get, but I'm willing to—"

"Knock knock," a feminine voice says as she pushes open the door and pokes her head inside. "I'd say I'll come back when you're done, but I've had to deal with this jackass firefighter all morning. And now I have to wait until they clear me to get back into the bakery. Opening day is *tomorrow*." The last word is practically a bark.

Smiling, I turn to face Marigold James, Love Beach's newest transplant and, hopefully, the baker of my parents' anniversary cake. Her bouncy brown hair gives her a girl-next-door look, but she's more sassy than sweet—something the *jackass firefighter* probably learned today.

Isaac's hands grip my waist and hold me in front of him, my back to his chest as his erection pokes me in the ass.

He wasn't kidding about being hard.

"All that from giving me a massage?" I ask playfully as I look at him out of the corner of my eye.

"You know what you do to me," he growls low in his throat as Marigold waves her hand at us.

"Still standing here," she says, her tone somewhere between amused and annoyed.

"What did you say the jackass firefighter's name was?"

"I didn't even get his name," she huffs as I sway my hips enough to have Isaac suppressing another groan.

My lips twitch both from the man behind me and the one that Marigold is undoubtedly talking about. "What does he look like?"

"Like a jerk," she says with an eye roll. "Styled blond hair, bulging muscles, and blue almost gray eyes." She scoffs. "And he called me ma'am! *Ma'am.* Do I look old enough to be a ma'am?"

Isaac stills behind me before he starts shaking with silent laughter. My smile widens as Marigold narrows her eyes at us.

"What's so funny?"

"It sounds a lot like Mads," Isaac says.

"Mads?"

"Maddox," I say as I wait for recognition to cross her pretty face, but it doesn't. "Maddox Baylor. He's my brother and more accurately my *twin.*" I pause and then state, "Older by fifty-seven seconds if you ask him."

"Oh, fuck a duck," she says. "I promise you guys can continue whatever rubdown foreplay that was going on as soon as I get my cider. Hell, I can just grab it myself; forget I was here," she grumbles with a flourish as she exits the way she came.

"I told you someone could walk in," Isaac says with a lopsided grin.

Shrugging, I move out of his hold. "Could have warned me."

"Where's the fun in that?"

Ignoring him, I make my way out into the main room and call to Marigold as she paces around. "Hold on, I already poured it; it's in the cooler."

"Thanks," she says as I hand her the cider with a smile, but she's already out the door before I can call after her.

"Think she and Mads are gonna get into it?" Isaac says from behind me, his hand grazing over my lower back as he comes to stand next to me. My gaze drops to the front of his jeans, and I'm sorry to see that he's gotten himself under control.

"I'd be surprised if they didn't," I say honestly with a shrug of my shoulder, my blonde ponytail swaying with the movement. Rolling my head from side to side, I marvel at how much better I feel after Isaac's fingers worked their magic on my neck and shoulders. Apparently, I'm a little out of shape for bartending and the general hustle of a night in Love Beach.

"She's not going to tell him, is she?" he asks casually, but I can hear the tremor of worry in his tone.

"Is there something to tell?" I tease Isaac as I turn and press my front to his side, his toned arm sandwiched between my breasts. He groans, and I can't help the twist of my lips. "What can it hurt?" I say, walking my fingers up the front of his shirt, reveling at the way his muscles flex beneath my touch. Teasing Isaac has always been a favorite pastime, but the fact that he's my boss is just an added bonus.

"We promised him, Reece," Isaac says as he grabs my wrist and forces my palm flat to his chest. "We promised your brother we wouldn't do this again."

We *had* promised Maddox back in high school when we'd started dating that if things didn't work out, we'd never be together again. He said he loved us both too much to go through it a second time.

At the time, it seemed like an easy promise to make. I'd had no intention of loving anyone else but Isaac for the rest of my life.

But with graduation came something I'd never accounted for, and our perfectly constructed plan exploded bigger than fireworks on the Fourth of July.

"He doesn't have to know," I tease, trying to keep the playful banter going even as his smile dims the slightest bit.

"You're going to have to be a lot quieter if we're going to pull this off," he murmurs as his gaze drops to my lips.

"Well then, don't leave the storeroom open next time."

"Next time, huh?"

"Just for the summer."

"Sounds like a terrible idea."

"Or it could be a lot of fun…" I let my eyes slide down his body. "I mean, how often does a girl get to sleep with her boss *and* her brother's best friend?"

2

ISAAC
ONE MONTH EARLIER

"Hey man, I need a favor," Maddox says, sliding onto the barstool next to me. We've been coming to The Cove Bar and Grill the last couple of years after looking around and realizing that we no longer fit in with the young college crowd at the Sandy Sipper.

I thought there'd be a mourning period, saying farewell to my youth, but *not a chance in hell*. Long ago were the days of sneaking off into dark corners for a hot kiss and a quick release—and really, it'd only ever been with one girl. We'd been wild and in love and absolutely crazy about each other. Letting her go had been hard, but knowing I'd never find anyone like her again had nearly been my undoing.

That and I'm sitting next to my best friend and her twin brother.

"Sure, what's up?" I ask as I take a sip of my beer.

"Reece is coming home, and she's bringing her friend Vienna. They're going to organize my parents' anniversary party."

"Yeah, she mentioned that," I say as casually as I can

muster, earning a side-eye from Maddox. Shrugging, I try and keep my face neutral as I say, "What? We still talk. We made a promise, and we kept it."

My voice is full of conviction as I utter the words, my enthusiasm masking the hurt that still lingers with missing having all of her.

He nods, acknowledging, but doesn't comment further. "Did she tell you they're coming back for the summer? My dad put in a good word for her at the high school here, but so far he said Reece hasn't made a decision. I think she likes her current job but..." He shrugs and I get it. Reece had texted me that she'd be here for the next few months. "I know you always need help with the summer crowd and was hoping you'd be able to give them jobs."

I try not to choke on my beer as I swallow the sip I'd taken and stare at him. He couldn't be serious. And yet, Maddox was almost always serious.

He didn't blink and neither did I because...

Shit.

Reece and I had been able to keep our hands to ourselves mainly because we hadn't been occupying the same zip code. And anytime she came to visit, I'd always made sure to take the seat on the other side of the living room or table to make sure my hand didn't find hers and *other things.*

Our breakup had hurt like hell, but it had been for the right reasons—for her at least. And I'd still do anything to make her happy.

"Yeah, I mean I usually hire some college kids, but they're not always reliable. Does Vienna have any bar experience?"

He nods. "I think they both worked at one of the bars when they were in school."

"And you were okay with that?" I ask, not bothering to hide my shock.

He shrugs, the movement stretching the fire department logo on his shirt. "She was gone, and I wasn't going to chase her down and bitch at her for missing curfew."

"That sounds exactly like something you would do."

He rolls his eyes. "Give me some credit. Besides, she made it pretty clear how she felt about me back then."

I don't say anything because I can't. Just like I can't be sure I didn't see the flash of hurt in his eyes at the admission. Still, his dismissiveness cuts deep—as if some asswipe college kid gets a free pass with Reece when I'd literally been wrecked over having to let her go.

Fuck your promise.

The words are on the tip of my tongue when Maddox turns his gray eyes on me, the usually stormy color filled with sincerity. "I know it was a long time ago, but thank you for standing by me—being here. I couldn't have done it without you. And I don't know if I ever apologized for the way things went down with Reece."

The fight drains from me in an instant because...he hadn't. Maddox's dream had always been to serve as a firefighter in Love Beach, and I'd lived through every grueling moment with him on the sidelines. He'd needed me, and I bottled all the heartbreak coursing through my veins and packed it away into the dark recesses of my soul.

"Of course." I hold my beer out to him, and he clinks his glass against mine. "I'll let Reece know that they have a job if they want it."

"Thanks, man. I'm real lucky to have you as my best friend."

"Yeah, well, who else would put up with you?"

He chuckles and shoves my shoulder. "Dick."

I return the sentiment, thankful for the distraction, all the while praying he'll still consider me his best friend after Reece leaves again, because having her in my bar—in my space—is going to take a whole lot of willpower I don't think I have anymore.

3

REECE

11 WEEKS TILL THE END OF SUMMER

"Sweetheart, I told you that you didn't have to plan anything for our anniversary," my mother says as she takes a pie from the oven. She's acting unaffected, but I know she's secretly pleased—it's not like my brother would have come up with the idea. Being married for thirty years is a big deal, and despite her passive-aggressive comments and displeasure at my chosen profession, I still want to do this for them.

"Like your mother said," my father says as he comes around the corner and places a kiss on my cheek, "we're just happy you're home for the summer." He raises an eyebrow as if to say *and maybe longer?*

"Well, I guess she has time to plan a party with her *schedule*."

It's amazing how much disdain one word can hold, as if being a high school biology teacher is something to be ashamed of.

"Yes, well, I'm still hoping I can rope Maddox into helping, considering you *just* gave me your guest list. I can't believe he took an extra shift tonight instead of coming to dinner."

My mother waves me off. "You know how busy your brother is. His job is so important, Reece, and he's in line for a promotion. He can't be worried about something so trivial."

Trivial.

This party or *me?*

My father gives me a sympathetic smile which I ignore because I could really use someone in my corner and not just silent support. My best friend, Vienna, won't be here until next week, and it feels like I'm on my own until then.

I shouldn't feel like a stranger in my hometown, but seven years feels like a lifetime since I spent any considerable time here. Even during my student teaching, I think my mother thought I'd "come to my senses" and follow in her footsteps.

Maddox had taken the easy way out, falling into the role of hometown hero and becoming a firefighter just like our father. So much of our time growing up was spent navigating the assumption that my brother and I would both fall in line.

He had but I hadn't.

It had just been too hard to correct every person I'd met who, well-meaning or not, had already decided my future for me.

And that included my brother, which probably hurt the most.

Maddox and I had been inseparable, but somewhere along the way I'd faded into the background, often blinded by the way he shined.

"Yes, well," I say as calmly as I can, "I guess I'll just take satisfaction in knowing that my *trivial* job is the one that prepares young minds and gives them a place for learning and personal growth so they can decide to go into such honorable professions."

"Oh, you know that's not what I meant," my mother huffs, but we both know it's exactly what she meant.

My father clears his throat as he takes the bowl of salad from me and guides me into the dining room. "John said he hasn't heard from you."

"I told him I would take some time to decide."

"You really should accept; your father put in a good word for you," my mom chides.

"Candee."

There's warning in his tone, but I've all but checked out as we take our seats. John Gomes had called me, and while I'd normally be racing to accept such a generous position, I couldn't take it knowing that my father had pulled strings to get me an interview.

"So, what kind of food were you thinking you'd like at the party? Cake? Or we can do cupcakes if you'd prefer," I ask a little too brightly before my first night back in Love Beach takes a turn we can't recover from. My father seems relieved as my mother launches into an animated description of a cake she'd seen recently in a magazine that would be *just wonderful* to celebrate their love.

Taking a breath, I paste a smile on my face and focus on the things I can control.

Like cake.

I love cake, and if this is the one thing my mother and I can agree on, I'll hold on to it with two hands and my last gasping breath.

4

ISAAC

"Is this seat taken?" a smooth, hypnotic voice asks me as I raise my glass to my lips. Goose bumps race over my body as if she'd touched me.

Because I know the girl that voice belongs to.

The woman, actually.

"It's yours."

The seat.

My heart.

My body.

Anything.

I wish I were being dramatic, but as I turn to look at my first and, really, *only* love, I can't imagine ever being as happy as I was with her.

"Thanks." She leans in and kisses my cheek, her hand gripping my forearm as she gets settled on the barstool.

"You look great," I say without thinking, but it's true because she always looks so damn good.

We'd been twenty when things had ended, and in the last seven years, she'd gone from the litheness of a beach-going college girl to a sun-kissed woman with curves and legs for days. There was no point in trying to get my hard-on under control. I was guaranteed to be like this for as long as Reece was in Love Beach.

"So do you," she says, giving me an appreciative look, her gaze dropping to my lap before snapping up to my face, a sweet pink coloring her cheeks. I fight the urge to adjust myself because that one quick perusal has me more worked up than any date I've been on since she's been gone.

The bartender places a beer in front of her, and I shake my head to clear the fog because *how did I miss her ordering a drink?*

"I like this place. I don't think I've ever really been in here," Reece says, looking around The Cove Bar and Grill, and I nod slowly because we'd never come here, choosing to spend most of our time at the beach or at the Sandy Sipper.

"Yeah, I just needed a little quiet tonight," I say, turning toward her, the motion shifting her crossed legs between mine.

It would be so easy to pull her into me—into my lap—and kiss her until I've erased all the years we've been apart.

"Me too."

"What happened?" I ask, pulling my head out of my ass and back to the present.

She gives me a wry grin and shrugs one shoulder. "I had dinner with my parents."

My hand grips my glass harder, and her lips quirk up on one side as she tracks the movement before meeting my gaze and giving me a full smile that completely steals my breath.

"Thanks," she says softly.

"I didn't say anything."

Nodding at the glass, she says, "You didn't have to." Taking a sip of her beer, she bobs her head from side to side.

"I just thought that they'd be proud of me by now, you know?" I open my mouth to speak, but she gives a humorless laugh. "They aren't. In seven years, nothing has changed. My brother is still the golden child, and my mother—ever doting on her hometown hero son—said that it was okay he missed dinner tonight because his job isn't as *trivial* as mine."

"Want me to kick his ass?" I offer. Even though he's not the whole problem, he'll have to do. She laughs, for real this time, but I'm not kidding. Best friend or not, I won't let Maddox hurt her, and honestly, he's being a chickenshit. He needs to stand up to their mother and end this weird rivalry she's created between them. Regardless of whether Maddox thinks it or not, he's hurt Reece by not speaking up. It's not like he can fix things by avoiding her the entire time she's in Love Beach.

Which isn't nearly long enough.

"No." Her fingertips trace over the scars on my hand, and I can feel that simple touch *everywhere*, my heart now hammering in my chest. "I don't want you to be in the middle."

Again.

The word hangs between us unspoken, but we'd all made choices that day, albeit for very different reasons.

Reece chose herself, Maddox chose me, and I—being the peacemaker—chose Maddox by default and lost my heart in the process.

My bar is my life, and it had always been my dream to take it over—make it mine—but there wasn't a day that went by that I didn't feel a twinge of regret too. The dream had turned bittersweet, and there was no salvaging it.

Not anymore.

"I know we talked about it," I say, swallowing hard and

then clearing my throat, "but are you sure you want to work for me?"

Reece frowns, her eyebrows pinching together as she stares at me. "You don't want me to?"

"What? No, of course I do, I just,"—*need to make sure I don't try and bend you over the bar top*—"want to make sure that's what you want."

"Yeah." She looks away quickly and then back at me. "It was one of Maddox's better ideas especially because it's only temporary. You won't have to train me too much, and I can vouch for Vienna."

The word *temporary* grates on me, but it's a necessary reminder that not everyone gets what they want in this scenario.

This summer.

Reece will be here just long enough to give me a taste of the life we could have had, and then she'll be gone and I'll... what, kick around Love Beach as a bachelor with Maddox forever?

The thought is terrifying and a little sad.

But what can I really do about it?

Does Reece even want a second chance?

The questions are unending, but one thing is clear—something's gotta give if I plan on surviving this summer with the one that got away.

5

REECE

9 WEEKS TILL THE END OF SUMMER

"What's next on the list?" Vienna asks as we walk down the sidewalk, my mood instantly brighter with her here. She'd been the first friend I made in North Carolina after I'd broken up with Isaac and momentarily destroyed my relationship with my brother.

She'd been there for me during the worst time of my life, and she'd never left my side.

"Can I just say how happy I am that you're finally in Love Beach?"

She chuckles and bumps her shoulder into mine. "I mean, you've told me twice today already, but by all means I'm listening."

Laughing, I let myself relax and enjoy the hot South Carolina weather and the humidity that won't quit. My soul is more relaxed this close to the ocean, even if my family is determined to give me an eye twitch to balance it out.

"You're amazing and I missed you."

"You are." She blows me an air kiss. "And..." she prompts, forcing me to roll my eyes.

"And...we've finalized the cake, DJ, venue...flowers maybe? I need to get the invitations sent out this weekend."

"Aren't you working a double both days?" she asks, pushing her sunglasses up on top of her head.

"Yeah, but it should be fine," I say, waving off her concern as I type out a text to my brother.

> REECE: Let's grab dinner and talk about Mom and Dad's anniversary party
>
> MADDOX: I'm working the next three days
>
> REECE: Okay...well maybe you can call me when you have some down time
>
> MADDOX: I'll text you
>
> REECE: I've barely seen you and while I'm happy to do most of the party planning I still need help
>
> MADDOX: I said I'll text you when I can—we just got a call I need to go
>
> REECE: Be safe I love you

I wait for a second and then growl when there's no return message before pocketing my phone.

"Brother?"

"Yes," I sigh.

"Tell him to stop being a dick. Or get Marigold on his case."

I snort. "Those two better make up their minds before they kill each other."

"I can't wait." Vienna laughs. "Honestly, it will be nice to see him put in his place."

"Shouldn't stop him from helping with the party though."

"Didn't he book the venue?"

"He did, but the parents of one of the guys he works with owns it, so it's not like he really slaved over finding something."

"True," she agrees emphatically, both because Mads needs to step up and as my best friend, she'll always side with me. "He should definitely help. And you know I will." Waggling her eyebrows, she adds, "I bet your boss would give you some time off if…" She pushes her tongue against her cheek, and I laugh and elbow her, causing her to stumble a little.

I can feel my face heat because I've had more than one fantasy about taking Isaac's cock to the back of my throat to see if I could still make him lose control. He'd been the first guy I'd ever been with, and I'd learned how to pleasure him —learning exactly what he liked and pushing the limits— exploring his body until he was sated and totally spent.

"Knock it off."

"What?" She feigns innocence. "I'm just saying you'd have to be blind not to see the sparks flying whenever y'all are within a hundred yards of each other."

I snort. "A hundred yards?"

"You're right. *Two hundred.* But seriously, why aren't you guys ripping each other's clothes off already?"

"You know why."

"Yeah, but it sounds like a stupid reason to me. You guys were young when you made that promise. You're adults and you shouldn't let your brother dictate your life. Isn't that why you moved away?"

I sigh because she's not wrong—not entirely at least. I'd never told Maddox the real reason I was leaving. He would have been crushed, and while I was upset with him, I still didn't want to hurt him.

Isaac had understood. The man was too damn nice. I'd broken us, but he'd taken the blame.

"But we're leaving at the end of the summer. Is it really fair to just hook up with him knowing it can never *just* be hooking up? Isaac and I have too much history for it to be a meaningless fling."

"Ahh." She hums knowingly. "So you have been thinking about it?"

"Of course I've been thinking about it," I hiss. "He knew every inch of my body back then, and he's *still* the most satisfying sexual experience of my life."

"Still? As in no one else has topped your high school boyfriend?"

"Nope." I pop the *p* for emphasis. "Not even close."

"Wow," she says with a low whistle, and I nod solemnly.

What good would it do to sleep with Isaac, have repeated, mind-blowing sex, and then leave knowing it would never be like that again?

"We leave in a matter of weeks, Vee. Do you really think it would be worth it?"

"Yes," she says without hesitation, something flickering in her gaze for only a second before it's gone. I don't mention it as we make our way to my car, nostalgia hitting me harder than I expected as I take in my hometown.

Love Beach looks different than I remember and yet exactly the same. I'd loved and hated being in a beach town growing up. The constant ebb and flow of tourists had been exciting, but I'd yearned for the quiet nights spent curled up with Isaac on the beach next to a bonfire.

"So, florist?" Vienna asks when we're tucking inside my car with the AC blasting, her question pulling me from my runaway thoughts.

"Yeah, but we'll have to go to the next town over. We still don't have one here."

Her eyes light up and she nods, forcing me to stare at her for a beat longer before shaking my head and putting the car in drive. I want to push her, but now's not the time. I just hope she knows I'm here when she's ready.

Turning up the music, I nod and sing along to the Descending North song blasting through the speakers and find Vienna doing the same.

No sense in worrying about it now. We'll have the rest of the summer to make the hard choices. I just hope they don't leave me heartbroken.

6

ISAAC

Walking over to the door, I flip the sign from closed to open and then turn to the bar with a smile. "All right, let's start the day!"

Vienna rolls her eyes, grumbling, "I'm already sick of this song," as she cues up "Cheeseburger in Paradise" by Jimmy Buffet.

"Blasphemy," I say with mock horror as Reece giggles and wipes down another glass. "Seriously, this is what sets us apart—what starts us on the right foot *and* pays tribute to one of the greatest musicians to grace the state of South Carolina."

Vienna blinks. "There is seriously something wrong with you."

"What? This is a classic," I say, doubling down with enthusiasm.

"Garth Brooks is a classic."

"And he's always welcome at Love Beach Brews,"—I point to the beach paraphernalia hung on the walls and the classic *here for a good time* vibe—"but salt water runs in our veins and sunshine is our caffeine."

"That's a metaphor. That's not actually real," Reece stage-whispers, earning my glare.

"Pretty sure you'd be dead with the salt water though," Vienna adds helpfully, her dark, wavy hair pulled up into a ponytail as her green eyes sparkle.

I huff, but there's no real heat behind it. Reece has always pushed my buttons, so it makes sense bringing her best friend here with her would exponentially increase the sass thrown my way.

I definitely don't hate it.

Already, the two of them had pulled in more tips during the weekday lunch rush than I had myself on a Friday night. I'm sure absolutely none of their middle school students learned anything with the two of them in the front of the class.

If I'm honest, I've had more than a few fantasies about Reece putting me in detention. With her dirty blonde hair and blue eyes, I've always been a goner for her. My heart lurches with the memory of how things ended between us, how I had to hide how much her leaving destroyed me.

But I'd promised Maddox—we both had—and until she showed up this summer, making Love Beach her temporary home again, I'd been able to keep that promise.

Loving her was easy.

It was her leaving that gutted me like a fish on the pier.

Still, my blood ran hot with every flirty smile Reece sent my way, every brush of her hand against mine, the way she bent over the bar giving me a peek down the front of her tank top with the Love Beach Brews logo on it.

Hell, I shouldn't want to rekindle things with her, but damn, it was tempting.

She'd always been tempting.

And I almost gave in last week in the storeroom, because

boy, did I want to, and if we hadn't been interrupted, there's no telling what would have happened. It had started innocently enough. She'd tweaked something in her back trying to get one of the boxes off the top shelf instead of waiting two minutes for me to help her.

She'd gotten it, but I'd come in just in time to see her grimace as she twisted back and forth trying to find some relief. I hadn't even thought about the consequences of offering to help alleviate the pain—I'd just wanted to help.

But the second my hands touched her body, I'd been transported back to the days that she'd been mine. My fingers kneaded and caressed her, and I'd been out of my mind with only that simple act. Marigold had been a blessing and a curse barging into the storeroom like she had because I wouldn't be able to resist my ex-girlfriend a second time.

And I didn't want to.

As the song winds down, Vienna escapes to the back to restock glasses or otherwise make herself scarce for the next twenty minutes. I don't know if she knows everything about my history with Reece, but she always seems to give us time alone when she can.

I should probably give her a raise.

"Hey Reece?"

"What's up?" she asks as she pauses slicing lemons to look at me.

"I was just wondering if you'd heard anything about the job at the high school."

"I haven't been able to get ahold of Mr. Gomes, but it was just an interview. I don't have any plans of moving back here."

It's a swift reminder of how fragile our relationship is here. I want her, and she's standing with one foot already out the door. We could joke and laugh about the past, and even if I know how good it would feel to get lost in her, I won't survive losing her again.

Hell, the hole in my heart never healed from the first time we said goodbye.

Reece's eyes plead with me to understand and I do.

Truly.

But I can't help wondering what our life would have been like if I'd gone with her—if I'd said to hell with Love Beach and taken a chance on us instead of running back home with a mangled heart.

The bell above the door chimes, and the moment's gone, just like my hope of making it through this summer with her here.

7

REECE

7 YEARS AGO

I let my eyes fall shut and will the tears not to fall as Maddox goes on and on about what comes next when the three of us return to Love Beach after finishing our associates degrees. He's excited. Animated. And he should be. He's getting to live his dream of following in our father's footsteps—becoming a firefighter and serving in our hometown.

"Isn't that great? And Mom is so excited about you getting into her alma mater for nursing school. It's crazy we're just like them, right? And it will be us in Love Beach again, like, this is it—what we've always wanted!" Maddox whoops, completely oblivious to the shell of myself I've become in the last two years.

"I'm not going," I whisper, the declaration like a record scratch in the room.

"What? Of course you are. It's just like we talked about, like you've always wanted," Maddox says, emphasizing the words even as confusion mars his face.

"It's what Mom wants—what *you* want—but no one ever asked me what I want!" Maddox freezes as he stares at me, his gaze bouncing between me and Isaac who is uncharacteristically quiet. I can't look at my boyfriend; I can't bear to see the hurt on his face.

"What are you saying?" my brother asks quietly.

"I'm saying that I got into the nursing program, but I also found a teaching program a few hours away that's incredible that I applied to." Steeling myself for the inevitable, I add, "And I was accepted."

"And you're..." Isaac's voice is pained like he can't get out the words, because he knows without me even saying it. It's over. *We're over.* Because I won't make him choose me over my brother.

Maddox would see it as a betrayal from Isaac if he followed me and I can't do that—to either of them.

"Not going back," I whisper. "I don't know if I ever will."

Isaac's eyes are glassy as they meet mine.

It's stupid but I know my brother better than I know myself, and we'd never survive this.

"So that's it?" Maddox practically yells over the silent communication I'm having with his best friend.

"It's what I want."

"But Love Beach is our home."

"I don't want to be a nurse, Mads. I don't want to be like Mom, and I don't want to go back home! I need more than Love Beach. I need more than just *being* in our hometown when no one actually sees *me*."

"You're going to throw everything away to be a *teacher*? You could be anything, Reece. And what about Isaac?"

"It's not throwing everything away! It's what I want; you're just not listening."

"And my best friend?" he says again as Isaac watches us.

"We will talk about it in private," I say as my boyfriend's eyelids flutter closed.

"How could you break us? This is bullshit!" Maddox yells, and it's the only thing that pulls Isaac back to the present as he stands and gets between us.

"Don't talk to your sister like that," he snaps, my brother's cheeks reddening as they stare each other down.

"If this is over," Maddox says, waving his hand between us, "then that's it. You're done. There's no sides, and you don't do this again. I was cool with it, but I won't stand by and watch you tear each other apart. Tear us apart. Not again."

"What? That's not—" Isaac starts but Mads cuts him off.

"You promised me." He looks around his best friend to me. "Both of you."

"Maddox."

"I'm serious, Reece. You guys want to ruin your relationship, that's on you, but this is it. There's no second chance after this. You promised me."

He's angry—angrier than I've ever seen him—but he's still my brother, and even though he's being a jackass, I still love him.

"Okay."

Isaac says the same and then it's just us left in my dorm room, the sound of the door slamming behind Mads deafening as we both stare at the inevitable end. It isn't until Isaac turns toward me, absolutely wrecked, that I lose it. Falling into his arms, I cry—we both do—as we mourn the end of us and the finality of promising never again.

8

REECE

8 WEEKS TILL THE END OF SUMMER

"Hey, Boss Man," I call as I give the bar top a final wipe down. Isaac pokes his head out of the back room and gives me an appraising look before glancing at the empty bar.

"Are you all set? Give me a second to finish this and I'll walk you out."

Swallowing down my nerves, I lean a hip against the cooler, his eyes tracking the sliver of skin between the top of my shorts and the hem of my tank, a sexy smile on my lips. "Wanna go for a walk on the beach?"

"Yeah." He licks his lips, his answer quiet but sure as he stares at me. My heart flutters in my chest before taking off at a gallop at the fact that I hadn't had to convince him at all.

"Really?"

"Always, Reece." His Adam's apple bobs as he nods toward the back. "Give me a few minutes and we can go."

We breeze through the closing routine, and before I can blink, Isaac has locked the door and tucked the keys in the pocket of his shorts. Lights all over Love Beach illuminate the night sky, and laughter carries on the breeze, and for once I don't hate it.

We walk along the familiar shore, the waves crashing softly on the sand. It's beautiful out even if it's still humid.

The silence between us is comfortable, and I slip my hand into Isaac's like I've done a thousand times. It's not my hand to hold, but I can't help myself, and if the way his fingers lace with mine is any indication, he can't either.

"I was thinking..." I start and he chuckles, his teeth white in the moonlight as he smiles at me.

"How much trouble are you going to get us in now?"

I shrug. "I don't know, but I don't think I care," I say, pulling us to a stop. He doesn't let go of my hand, instead twisting it behind me so our interlocked fingers rest on my lower back, his other palm cradling on my hip.

"No?"

"No." He teases the hem of my shirt, the roughness of his skin against the smoothness of mine. "I can't stop thinking about that day, and *God,* do I want that again. But more."

"I've never been so turned on by massage in my life," he rasps.

"Me either. I missed you so much."

"But you're leaving," he says while dragging me until we're pressed together, chest to chest all the way down to our toes, my back arching just so I can meet his gaze.

"And we could have an incredible summer."

"I hated letting you go once already. It still hurts, Reece."

"I know."

"So what are we gonna do? Just flirt and fuck and say goodbye when our time comes to an end?"

He meant the words to be harsh, but I can't deny the way hearing him say *fuck* has my panties absolutely soaked. His cock is hard between us, and I rock my hips against him to make sure he knows how badly I want him.

"I know it's going to hurt when I leave, but I can't be close to you every day and not feel your hands on me." His lips ghost over my pulse utterly hammering in my throat, my eyelids fluttering shut as I squeeze my thighs together, unabashedly desperate for him.

"God, Reece, you feel so damn good, but we shouldn't—"

"I don't care that we shouldn't. Just tell me that you want to," I beg as he trails hot, open-mouth kisses along the underside of my jaw, forcing me to tilt my head back with a gasp and a moan.

"You know I want to." His tongue follows the same path as his lips, pulling my earlobe between his teeth and nibbling enough to make me squirm.

"Then take me home, strip me down, and spread me wide, Isaac. Make me scream your name."

"Fucking hell," he groans a second before his lips crash over mine, his hand on my hip moving to grip my ass and grind me against the hardness of his erection. Isaac's tongue teases the seam of my lips with one quick swipe before plunging inside my mouth and ravaging every available inch.

He tastes like mint and smells like the faintest bit of sunscreen, but mostly, he smells like *him*—the way he always has—comfort warring with lust as he releases my hand to grip my ass and pull me up his body. My fingers tangle in his hair, pulling and angling him closer until he's cursing into my mouth, carrying me and stumbling up the path to the main road.

We'd done the sex in the sand thing exactly one time our senior year, and there had been no orgasms that night until after we'd thoroughly rinsed off because...*ouch*. Some people might have mastered that, but we'd been too frantic and had no desire to try again. I want to laugh at the memory, but the anticipation of finally having him inside me is too overwhelming.

Isaac stops at the top of the path and lets me slide down his body. "I should have gotten you off at the beach."

"Make it up to me at your house," I breathe, gripping his hard-on through the soft fabric of his shorts.

"Think we'll make it?" he asks, already pulling me along, his fingers tightening around mine.

"Definitely there," I tease, making him turn his head to look at me, "but I can't make any promises as to what will happen as soon as the door closes behind us."

"Well, I can, and I can assure you, you're gonna have a hard time walking tomorrow."

"You say the sweetest things, Isaac Nowak."

"You haven't heard anything yet. Now get your sweet ass in the car before I fuck you against it."

"That's not the threat you think it is," I sass, but he just glares as he rips my door open and nudges me inside.

"And there's no way I'm going to give anyone the chance to see what's mine spread and soaking wet and taking my cock." My lips part at the audacity and the *visual* as a devilish smirk settles across his. "Not yet at least."

I gasp and he chuckles as he slams my door and rounds the front of the car.

Isaac has always been my kryptonite, but right now he looks like my favorite kind of trouble.

9

ISAAC

The ride back to my house is quick and blessedly quiet, and I try—and fail—to calm the inferno inside me. Reece Baylor is set on putting me into an early grave, either from a heart attack being this turned on or from her brother finding out about us breaking a teenage promise.

She squeezes her legs together in the passenger seat and shifts again, sealing my fate, as if there'd ever been any doubt. No, I'll die a happy man just having my face buried between her thighs one more time.

Although, I pray it will be more.

Turning into the driveway on autopilot, the car is barely in park before Reece's door is open and she's stepping out onto the pavement.

I growl, fighting my seat belt and sending it slamming back into place with an audible thud, then push out into the sticky night air.

"Better hurry," Reece whispers as she whips her tank top over her head, hitting me in the face with the black fabric. The shadows of the house hide her from the road but not from me. Black lace cups—because lace has always been her favorite—push her tits up high, practically forcing them to spill over the top.

"You're just begging to get off out in the open, aren't you?" I ask, stalking over, caging her against the side of the house so she's forced to look up at me, exposing the long line of her neck all the way down her body. Her chest heaves, her skin gloriously sun-kissed, those luscious tits begging for my mouth and that lace barely hiding the pale pink nipples I missed so much.

"Is this what you want?" I ask, popping the button on her cutoff jean shorts and dragging the zipper down. "Right here where everyone will hear the second you come all over my fingers? Because I know you, Reece. You can try to be quiet—hell, sometimes you get real close—but you *always* get loud." My fingers slip over her lace-covered clit and she gasps. She's soaked, and I want to thrust inside all that wet heat with my fingers, my tongue, and my cock until she forgets her own name.

"Isaac, please," she whispers, her hands fisting my shirt as she tries to pull me closer, but I won't let her. Not this time. She wants to scream for my neighbors, and I'll make sure they know exactly who made her lose control.

"You did always like getting a little wild, didn't you, Baby?" Bracing one arm over her head, I keep my mouth close to hers as I slide my fingers up and down her slit, pressing and circling before moving down again.

"I want your hands on me," she whines, her hips bucking against my barely there ministrations.

"No, you wanted to taunt me, putting your tits on display for anyone to see."

"Just you."

"If I have to suffer," I say, dipping my finger barely under the edge of her panties and dragging it through her wetness, "then so do you."

Letting go of my shirt, she tries to arch her back, her hands moving to unclip her bra, but I catch her wrists in my palm, pinning them over her head.

"I can't wait to have you on your knees," I vow, and she whimpers as I thrust into her core, the heel of my hand pressing and grinding against her clit. "You always took my cock so good between those pouty pink lips."

"Isaac." She fights my hold, her breathing ragged as her orgasm builds.

"You're gonna let me fuck into your sweet mouth, aren't you?" Her pupils are wide and she nods frantically. "You're gonna let me do anything I want to you, and you're going to be *begging* me to let you come."

"Yes!" She moans loud enough to draw attention as I crook my fingers just right inside her before slamming my mouth against hers. Her walls clamps down around me, and I swallow every scream and whimper and every breath as she rides out her release.

"Fuck, that was hot," I growl as I pull back and let go of her arms. Reece sags against the house, and my expression is wolfish as I lean forward and lick the drop of sweat running down into the valley of her breasts.

"Oh God," she whispers, arching her tits into my face and yanking at my hair.

"You'll have plenty of time to talk to him later," I tell her, gripping her ass and lifting her off the ground.

"I couldn't wait," she admits, partially an apology for demanding my hand down her pants next to the shrubbery when literally two steps would have taken us inside the privacy of my home.

"Well," I say, pushing the key into the lock and turning the handle before carrying her over the threshold, "I hope it was worth it because I wasn't kidding about getting you on your knees." I drag her center over my cock, my erection incredibly hard and intent on satisfaction, and she gasps. "You did that, Reece, and now...you're going to take care of it."

10

REECE

Oh sweet baby Jesus in a manger.

Isaac's eyes are predatory as he drops me onto his bed, having kicked the door closed with his foot before stalking through the house to his room. I want whatever this is—whatever he wants to give me.

And it want it now.

As I move my hand behind my back to take my bra off, he shakes his head again. "Just your shorts," he growls. Surprise and another wave of anticipation roll through me, and he smirks. "You wore the set for me, didn't you? Be rude not to let me enjoy it."

My heart hammers in my chest because *I did* wear this set for him. I'd bought it before Vienna and I had come to Love Beach, and I hadn't worn it before tonight because I was kidding myself if I thought it was for anyone but him.

Myself included.

I never bought lingerie for a man. I always bought it for me, because when our time together was over, I didn't want to sully the garment with the memory of something that didn't last.

But Isaac was always the exception.

And honestly, these panties might be ruined after tonight anyway considering how thoroughly I'd soaked them.

"Ah, dark blue," he praises, his lips curling up into a devilish smile, finally noticing the set isn't black like it looked outside. "My favorite."

"I know," I admit as I shimmy the denim over my hips and down my legs. "I bought it for you."

Surprise flares in his eyes, the blush creeping from my chest all the way up to my face before he's gripping my ankles and dragging me to the edge of the bed.

Dropping to the floor in front of me, he pushes my thighs wider. "After I feast on this drenched pussy, I'm going to feed you my cock. Do you understand?"

"Yes," I moan as he pulls my panties to the side, the roughness of his fingers and the friction of the lace against my clit making me practically see stars.

"I tried to be so good, Reece. I tried, but now I'm going to ruin you for anyone else. I'm going to fuck your sweet mouth and then make you come apart again before sinking my cock inside you. Do you want that?"

"Please," I beg because who wouldn't? The man is possessed and completely unhinged with desire—for me. Dropping his head, he licks, sucks, teases, and builds me to a height I won't survive the fall from. I don't tell him that I'd been ruined for every other man the first time he kissed me when we were sixteen.

I shatter, and he licks me harder, his tongue spearing inside me, forcing my back to bow off the bed as I come again, screaming his name. No one has ever done this to me, and I know deep in my soul that no one else ever will.

"So fucking beautiful," Isaac says, pulling my panties

over my sensitive flesh and climbing over me to drop an indecent kiss on my lips.

His hand coasts over the side of my breast, and I shiver as I reach to cup his erection. He grunts and thrusts into my touch.

With a seductive smile and gentle push against his chest that lands him with his back on the mattress, I kneel between his legs with my fingers working the button on his shorts. "My turn."

11

ISAAC

"*Babe.*" I stir at the whispered word, and even though the sun is up, I sure as hell don't want to be. We opted to sleep at her place last night, only because Vienna wouldn't be home until later today. Their summer rental is bright and airy, complete with obligatory beach theme. I'd probably be more judgmental of the décor, but I haven't slept this well in years. Although I'm sure it has more to do with the girl in my arms than the accommodations.

"Go back to sleep," I murmur into Reece's hair as my arms tighten around her. I may not be awake, but my cock is and it's hard against her ass. She wiggles back and I groan, my hand coming up to cup her breast, pinching her nipple between my fingers.

She's probably sore, but you'd never know it the way she's rocking against me and moaning my name.

Knock. Knock. Knock.

We both freeze, not daring to move, like if we stay perfectly still, whoever it is will go away.

Knock. Knock. Knock.

"Sissy! Why is the door locked?" Maddox calls out, and I

bite back the groan that wants to escape while visions of killing my best friend dance through my head.

"Shit!" Reece screeches, jumping out of bed and spinning around, gloriously naked. With her perky tits and chest flushed, she's absolutely stunning. "Oh my God, get dressed! What are you doing?!"

"What?" I ask and she glares, but it's her fault because she's sexy and I'm easily distracted when she's naked.

"Hide in the closet or something!" she hisses, grabbing her robe off the back of the bedroom door and slipping it on and glaring at me.

"What? No. I'm not hiding in the closet—just get rid of him."

"Oh sure, no problem, just answering the door wearing nothing but a robe, talking to my brother while his best friend lies naked in my bed. Easy peasy."

My lips twitch as I prop my hand behind my head, my eyes dragging down over her body. "Tell him you were about to take a shower and then come back so you can ride me."

I let my other hand drift under the sheet to grasp my cock, stroking it lazily for emphasis and earning a little growl from Reece.

Spinning on her heels, she opens the bedroom door and then closes it behind her, her footsteps disappearing down the hall.

Staring up at the ceiling, I practically groan when I hear Mads in the kitchen. Their voices are muffled, but it's obvious he's hunting around for a snack. Any other time, I'd be happy he's trying to be more present with Reece, but she's naked and *I'm naked* and fuck if I don't want her back in this bed.

I take a breath, looking around the room, her clothes thrown haphazardly over the chair in the corner. It's a mess, but it makes me smile because she's still my Reece. Photos and perfume line the dresser, a single photo jammed into the frame of the mirror.

It's faded and the edges are curled, but I know exactly what day that was taken, and it has my heart squeezing a little in my chest. Mads, Reece, and I stand on the beach with our arms wrapped around each other, heads thrown back in laughter our junior year of high school.

It was a great day, one I look back fondly on even now.

And apparently Reece does too.

Rolling onto my side, I grab my phone from the nightstand and stop short when I realize that Reece's isn't there. She must have grabbed it without me noticing.

Perfect.

Honestly, I shouldn't mess with her. I really shouldn't.

But it's too tempting not to.

Putting one hand back behind my head, I pull the sheet down over my hip and flex before snapping a picture and sending it to Reece.

It's marked as *delivered* and then *read,* and when Maddox doesn't come busting through the door, I reach my hand under the sheet and stroke my cock with one hand. Making sure I get my abs, my hand going under the sheet and the print of my erection against the cotton, I take the picture and grin.

She's going to kill me, but it's going to be so worth it. Maybe I can convince her to try and suffocate me while she rides my face.

This time the text is *delivered* but not *read.*

Worrying my bottom lip with my teeth, I debate my options. I could send her a dick pic, but I feel like that's not as fun. On the other hand, I'm running out of creative ways to flex my abs. Throwing one leg out of the covers, I take one last picture and hit send before tossing my phone on the bed beside me.

And wait.

And wait.

By the time I hear Reece usher Maddox out the door, my nerves are shot, and the need to have her in my arms again is overwhelming. I hate lying to my best friend, but Reece has always been the absolute light of my life, and if I only have a few weeks with her, I'm gonna make damn sure to make it count.

Her footsteps quicken as she reaches the bedroom, her hand turning the knob with such force the door flies open and bangs against the wall.

"What the hell was this? Were you trying to get us caught? Or just give me a heart attack?" Reece waves her phone at me before tossing it on the dresser and wrestling with the tie on her robe.

"I just wanted to see how wet and needy I could make you."

"You're a jerk," she says sweetly, climbing onto the bed and crawling toward me.

"You should have gotten rid of him faster," I bite out as she places hot, open-mouth kisses all over the head of my cock through the sheet. "Turn around." Her eyes flash to mine, defiant and turned on and so damn beautiful. "Do it, Reece. I want to lick your sweet pussy while you suck my cock."

"I'm a little obsessed with how filthy your mouth is."

"Yeah?" I grin wolfishly as I pull her up my body, brushing my lips against hers in a barely there kiss. "I'm more than a little obsessed with how your mouth looks wrapped around my dick."

"Bossy."

"You fucking love it," I goad, bringing my palm down on the curve of her ass, making her yelp and then moan, before rubbing herself against me when I do it again. "Later," I murmur, giving her ass one final squeeze. "Right now, I need you to climb up here because I'm starving."

12

ISAAC

7 WEEKS TILL THE END OF SUMMER

"So how are things goin' with Vienna and Reece working at the bar?" Maddox asks as we walk into The Cove Bar and Grill, bypassing the tables and grabbing two stools at the end of the bar.

We smile as a bartender I don't recognize drops two coasters and menus in front of us, before taking our drink order and disappearing blessedly from sight. I need to gather myself because even though I knew I'd have to face Maddox at some point, I also couldn't put into words how right it felt having Reece in my bed every night this week.

But it's not just about the amazing sex or the insane chemistry between us—it's the way we stay up and talk for hours about everything and nothing. It's the way she's crawled inside me and claimed a piece of me without even trying.

And it's the way I can't shake the feeling I might do something crazy to keep her.

"They're doing great," I say as casually as I can manage as the bartender drops off our beers. "It's nice to have the help."

"That's good and I appreciate it," he says, taking a sip. I take one too, swallowing my grimace thinking of how much he *would not* appreciate the things I did to Reece last night.

Or how he'd burst into her apartment when we'd still been naked in bed.

Being with her in high school had been one thing. We'd been young and tentative, and even though things had gotten heated as we got older, it was nothing compared to the way we devour each other now.

I shift, and the bite mark she left on my inner thigh last night while she gifted me the most earth-shattering blow job of my life rubs against the seam of my shorts, and I barely stop a grunt from escaping.

Taking another sip of my beer, I blow out a heavy breath and will my ass to relax. The last thing I need is Maddox getting suspicious, but more than that, I don't want to accidentally alienate my best friend because I can't keep my shit together.

Looking at him, I'm startled to see the way he's focused on the condensation on his glass, his forearms braced on the bar top.

"You okay, man?" I ask, my eyebrows furrowing the longer I look at him.

"It's this girl, man...she's driving me crazy."

"Marigold?" His gaze whips to me, and I hide my smirk behind my glass.

"How do you know that?"

"She came into the bar for cider and was talking about the cocky, hot firefighter." I shrug. "Reece was there working and we were able to narrow it down pretty quick." I pause. "Also, you know she and Reece are friends, right?"

He grumbles something under his breath. "She's fucking

chaos and she doesn't want my help, but her damn shop is setting off the alarm every damn day."

"Did you use your charming voice? Women always like that." He glares at me and I chuckle. "Okay, so if charming didn't work, did you try *nice?* Sometimes you forget that one."

"Of course I was nice. I'm always nice." My eyebrows creep up my forehead and he sighs. "Every time I see her I just..." He sighs. "Something about her makes me want to pick a fight, every damn time. Doesn't matter what it's about, I just want to get a rise out of her."

"It sounds like you have a thing for Love Beach's newest shop owner." He opens his mouth and then closes it again, the warring inside him obvious. "Maybe you should just go talk to her. No pretenses—just have a conversation and go from there."

"Maybe," he admits and I nod, slapping him on the shoulder and eliciting a grunt and a scowl.

"That's the spirit."

Polishing off my beer, I set my glass on the bar and throw enough money down to cover our drinks.

"Where you headed?" he asks even though I know his mind is still stuck on a certain cake baker with girl-next-door looks and a sassy mouth.

"I'm taking Reece and Vienna to the Book & Barrel." This gets his attention as he gawks at me.

"What did you do to deserve that?" he asks incredulously.

"I lost a bet," I admit with a shrug and a grin.

"You lost a bet, and now you need to take my sister and her best friend to the bookstore?"

"Yep," I say, popping the *p* and shoving my hand in my front pocket as I stand. "I owe them each a book too."

"What the hell kind of bet did you make?" He laughs, his expression filled with amusement, and I'm happy he's at least distracted for a moment.

"They bet me that they could kick the keg on the English Breakfast Tea Stout running a special with Choco-Love pairing chocolates."

"That's a good one. Did Noah make it?"

I nod. Noah Drake and I hadn't socialized too much over the years, but I had to admit the guy was something of a genius when it came to chocolate.

"Dark chocolate truffles with a dark, sweet, cherry in the middle surrounded by a raspberry cream filling and edible gold sprinkled over each one. Have you ever seen edible gold? It was insane."

"That is *very* specific," Maddox says with a wry grin.

"I said it so many times it's burned into my brain. I also walked over there as soon as they opened the next day and asked for a box for myself."

And Reece.

But I don't say that part out loud.

"And how long did it take for the girls to win?"

"We didn't even make it to eight o'clock," I say, thinking back to how everyone had raved over the idea. It had been a hit, and I'd already talked to Noah about a repeat event.

Maddox snorts and shakes his head. "So now you owe them a drink and a book?"

"Yeah,"—I glance down at my watch—"and now I gotta run."

"Have fun with that." He snorts into his beer, but I can't help but grin.

Oh, I plan to.

13

ISAAC

"I cannot believe you agreed to this," Vienna says as we walk the short distance to the Book & Barrel, the former church turned bar and bookstore. It's a nice night, and the large bay doors are open, laughter spilling out into the street.

"What? I brew beer so I can't like wine?" I ask with faux irritation as Vienna rolls her eyes. She has siblings, and because I know she's missing hers, I try my best to be as annoying as I can.

Because I'm nice like that.

"I'm just saying this seems a little...high-class for your beach-bum taste. You give off more of the beer-helmet vibe."

I chuckle, letting her and Reece walk in front of me toward the bar. They're in sundresses and the platform sandals that women somehow just *know* how to walk in without risk of serious injury.

Even though they're only supposed to be here for the summer, both of them brought enough shoes to last a year. I doubt I've had that many shoes in my entire life. It's probably a bad comparison though because my lame sneakers are no match for the sexy as hell wedges with ribbon tied up both Reece's calves.

And I can't wait to fuck her with them on.

The place is chic but still cozy with its mix of tables and inviting white leather chairs. The owner, Vivian, kept so many of the original elements, accentuating the cathedral ceilings and the stained glass windows in the front instead of hiding or replacing them. Bookshelves line the space, but my favorite thing is that you can only get wine, tap water, or sparkling water here.

That's it.

And tourists and locals alike can't get enough.

Sam is behind the bar, and she nods at us as we approach. "What can I get you?"

The girls order glasses of white wine and I do the same, though, truth be told, I'd rather have a beer.

Sliding my card across the bar, I motion for Sam to keep it open as Reece and Vienna gush over her bangs and the more red than brown color of her hair. It's...strange. There's never a shortage of conversations like these at my bar, but I've never had a reason to really pay attention.

But I could sit here and listen to it all night, because this is the closest thing to a date I could take Reece on without Maddox being suspicious. She's happy and so am I.

For now.

My heart squeezes at the thought of losing her after it feels like a part of me has come alive in the last few weeks she's been home.

Sam tells them about the book club the bar runs, and I watch as Vienna and Reece nod enthusiastically, talking about whatever the upcoming read is, the details sending my eyebrows into my hairline.

It sounds...spicy. But hell, if a book club with a variety of smutty books would keep my girl in Love Beach, I'd buy every single one for her.

Thanking Sam for their drinks, the girls move around the bar, sliding between patrons to peek at the bookshelves. Reece winks at me over her shoulder, and I feel that simple acknowledgment like a physical caress. Nothing about being with her feels temporary; it just feels *right*.

And the longer I let this go on, the harder it will be to let her go. Thoughts of selling the bar or maybe opening a second location close to where Reece lives flit through my head, the latter taking hold with enthusiasm.

It's crazy.

But not that crazy.

Taking a sip of my wine, I stare at the glass in horror as I swallow the cool, crisp liquid. It's delicious. Shamefully so, and I instantly feel like I'm cheating on my brews down the street while also wondering if I can get a bottle of this to go.

"It's good, right?" Reece's eyes sparkle as she watches me, taking a sip of her own drink.

"I really hate that I like it," I admit.

"I can see that." She laughs. "What do you think about this one?" Reece asks, holding up a book with a ripped, sweaty guy on it.

"I think I should probably start hitting the gym," I say, looking down and patting my abs through my short-sleeve Henley. Reece picked it out, admitting she liked how the seafoam-green color looked against my tan.

Giving me a wicked smirk, she steps into me, placing her hand on my chest and popping up on her tiptoes to whisper in my ear.

"I licked every dip and line of your abs last night. I think you're doing just fine."

Suppressing the groan, I wrap my arm around her back

and pull her flush against me, her eyes dancing with amusement.

And lust.

"You can lick a lot more than my abs tonight with that mouth."

She giggles, but I'm not kidding.

Not even a little.

"Y'all know you can't whisper, right?" Vienna says, eyebrow raised and lips quirked as she pretends to read a random page in the book she's holding.

"Man, she's nosy," I say, burying my face in the crook of Reece's neck.

"Um, not nosy, just standing here."

"We need to find her a man," I tease, pulling back to look at Reece, but Vienna snorts and shakes her head.

"I'm doing just fine, Nowak. Don't you worry about me."

"What?!" Reece hisses, lightly smacking Vienna on the arm. "You're seeing someone and you didn't tell me?"

"*Seeing someone* is kind of a stretch. We're just hooking up." She shrugs.

"Hey, good for you," I say, earning a smirk from Vienna and a glare from Reece.

"Who is he? Where did you meet him?" Reece presses, and I stifle a laugh as Vienna closes the book, tucking it into her arm before pulling another from the shelf.

"I went to visit my sister, and she took me out in Magnolia Point and I met a guy."

"And? Oh my God, why are you making me pry this out of you?"

"Stop being so dramatic. We met, we talked, we hooked up, and decided that hooking up until he moves at the end of the summer is perfect for both of us."

"Are we going to meet him?" Reece asks with a huff, making Vienna narrow her eyes at her.

"What? No. Why would you meet him? I'm not dating him, Reece. We're just engaging in mutually beneficial orgasms." Reece opens her mouth and then closes it as Vienna's expression softens. "Sweetie, it's okay that that's not you."

"Damn straight it's not you," I growl and pull Reece tight against my side.

"Y'all are disgusting, but I love you."

"I've never appreciated anyone more than in this moment," I say, my tone amused, but I'm serious. Vienna has kept our secret, and it's been nice not to have to pretend around her.

"That's gonna cost you another book, Nowak."

"Sold."

She smirks but I just shrug, taking another sip of my wine because I'll take a thousand nights like this over a lifetime with anyone else.

Like she's reading my mind, Reece turns and places a lingering kiss on my cheek. "Thank you for the perfect night."

"It's perfect because you're in it."

"Aaaand now you owe me three books," Vienna says with a wave over her shoulder as she moves farther down the shelves. "I'll be over here when you're done being gross."

"It's amazing you're friends," I say on a laugh, but I'm not serious. In fact, I'm so damn thankful that they've had each other all these years and that I get to now be privy to the chaos they create.

Add Marigold into the mix, and those three are bound to get into trouble in Love Beach. My smile falls because it's just one more thing—one more person—she'll be leaving when the summer ends.

14

REECE

"I wish I could take you out on a real date," Isaac whispers in the darkness, his fingertips running up and down my spine, a shiver chasing the movement.

"Tonight doesn't count?" I tease, trying to lighten the mood. We'd had a great time with Vienna at the Book & Barrel, but it wasn't the same.

Not even close.

"You know what I mean."

"Maybe we should," I say even though it lacks conviction. A promise we made years ago shouldn't hold so much weight but it does.

Turning my head, I meet his gaze, the moonlight creeping in through the gap in the blinds. He's so handsome it hurts. The boyish features I'd fallen for have been replaced with strong angles and cut muscles, but his eyes—his eyes are the same glorious dark-amber color that I'd lost myself in time and time again.

"If you were staying," he starts, swallowing the obvious hurt before continuing, "I wouldn't hesitate. But I don't think it's worth it for either of us to have to deal with the fallout if it's only for a few more weeks." His voice is barely a whisper as he adds, "I wish I could get you to stay."

I wish that too, but I don't know if I could let myself come back here—even if I want to. What Isaac and I have is incredible, but how long until I become the same girl in this beach town that I was all those years ago?

And he's right.

Even though my brother is being unbearable right now, he'd be devastated if he knew we messed around only for me to pack my stuff up at the end of the summer again.

"Nothing else has changed, Isaac." I sigh defeatedly. "My mother is unable to hide her disdain for, well, everything I do, and my brother is so wrapped up in his own head he can't see what's going on around him."

"We can handle your mother," he says quietly.

"But what about Mads? He needs to find some balance, and I can't do that for him. He's gone from obsessing about fire to obsessing about fire and Marigold, and while I'm happy for him, he's a loose cannon."

"I can handle him."

"But you shouldn't have to," I whisper, pressing a soft kiss to Isaac's lips. "I love him, but seven years didn't erase all the reasons I couldn't come back here."

"Maybe Marigold will soften him up," Isaac says, trying for levity.

"It would help having her on our side, especially considering she knows about us," I say, looking past him at the wall for fear I'll admit I can't live without him and beg him to move with me.

"Well, she kind of caught us in the storage room."

"But I mean she *knows*."

"Did you tell her?"

"I didn't have to."

"Is she going to tell Mads?"

"Of course not."

"How do you know?"

"He's so focused on her he can't see what's going on around him. That's on him, not us, and besides, it's girl code."

"Girl code?"

"Yeah. And it's not fair that he can be open about wanting my best friend, but I can't do the same in return."

"I thought Vienna was your best friend."

"She is, but Marigold is too. We clicked, and no matter what happens, I know that we'll always be like that."

Isaac stares at me unconvinced, but it's true. Marigold was a bright spot to coming back to Love Beach, and our friendship has been easy right from the start.

"So, what do we do?" I ask, startling myself that I'd said the words out loud.

Isaac studies me for a moment, before pushing up and settling his body over mine. Even after so much time apart, the man knows me better than I know myself.

He's an anchor in the storm brewing inside me.

My anchor.

My chest squeezes at the thought of leaving him again, at packing up and moving away from the town I've come to love again.

Away from him.

My face must give something away because before I can take my next breath, Isaac's mouth is on mine, his kiss bruising and all-consuming as he presses me into the mattress.

"Let go, Reece. Give me every second till you're gone."

15

REECE

"Um wow, okay," Vienna says as she looks at the absolute disaster laid out over the living room of our rental.

Blowing out a breath, I nod. "Yeah, I know." Poster board, favors, sticky-note reminders for the seating chart, and decorations litter every available surface.

"I saw your brother and Marigold getting cozy at the bar last night," she says as she drops onto the couch and tucks her feet under her.

"Yeah, they're both too damn stubborn for their own good."

"I don't know anyone like that," Vienna deadpans, and I glare at her because it's not the same. Marigold had a lot of baggage from her asshole ex, and my brother continued to just be an asshole.

But he was getting better.

Especially with us finally being able to wrap up the plans for the party, the mess in front of me aside. It feels like I can finally breathe again—maybe enjoy the rest of summer.

And it was obvious last night how much my brother cares about Marigold, but love and lust don't fix your problems no matter how hard you try. I just hope he figures it out before it's too late.

"What's that face for?"

"Just hoping my brother can figure his life out before he loses Marigold. She's so sweet and fun and everything he needs. We've gotten close, and honestly, if they don't work out I'm keeping her"—I pause—"and Logan, the guy who works with her; he's a hoot."

"I met him the last time I stopped into Cakeology." Vienna laughs and give me some serious side-eye. "But I'm your best friend."

"I can have more than one best friend."

"I don't like it."

I roll my eyes. "Are you going to see Aspen this weekend?"

"Kind of. I mean I'll see her but..."

"You're going to hook up with the guy you won't tell me any details about?"

"There's nothing to tell."

"You can ask about me and Isaac and I'll tell you."

She snorts and starts assembling a pile of the favors. "Girl, I hear you guys through the walls—there's *nothing* I don't already know."

My mouth drops open and my face flames. I stare at her for a whole ten seconds before she falls over, laughing hysterically, tears leaking from her eyes.

"I cannot believe you just said that."

"What? It's true. And, if I may, that sounds like a forever kind of love."

"Please stop talking," I say as I cover my face with my hands and will my cheeks to return to their normal color.

"In other news," she says, making me peek from between my fingers, "I need to tell you something, and I hope you won't be mad."

"Of course I won't be mad." My hands drop as I give her my full attention. "Besides, I'm still mortified, so you've got that going for you." She smiles but it doesn't totally meet her eyes.

"I'm staying in Love Beach."

"What? Really?" I ask, a surge of surprise and *hope* flooding through my veins. Because if she can do it...

"I already put in my notice at work."

"But you love teaching."

"I do, but I just don't feel that spark anymore, and I know it doesn't make sense but ever since we got here I just... I feel like it's where I'm supposed to be."

My lips can't fight the grin stretching over my face. "Tell me."

Blowing out a breath, Vienna squares her shoulders as she looks at me. "This town has everything but a flower shop..."

"I knew it!" I fist pump in the air, making her lips twitch.

"And I've always loved them—even when I was little, I always had a garden. My brother paid off my student loans, and with the money I've saved and the tips from this summer, I think I'll have enough soon to put a down payment on one of the vacant storefronts."

I can't help it. I squeal and launch myself at her, wrapping my best friend in an enthusiastic hug. "Oh, I'm so proud of you!" She laughs but hugs me back tight, her eyes glassy when she pulls back to look at me. "And you have a name; I know you do."

"The Greene House."

"Oh my gosh, it's perfect! Vienna *Greene,* fabulous and

brilliant owner of The Greene House!" I deliver the line with a flourish.

"Exactly like that." She chuckles. "There's a guy that lives a town over from where I grew up who is friends with my brother and a genius with plants. He made his own self-sustaining greenhouse, and I'm hoping if I can make this happen that he'll build me one."

"Of course, you're going to make it happen, and I'm going to help you—whatever you need."

"And what about you?" she asks with a slight cock of her head.

Blowing out a breath, I study my hands in my lap before meeting her gaze. "I have a meeting with the principal at the high school here. Our schedules haven't aligned, and I just..."

"Want to make sure they want *you*?"

"Yes," I whisper. Because I can't stay if my father really did call in a favor.

"They do. And then you and Isaac can finally be together," she says, squeezing my hand. "Aaaand then you can tell Maddox."

Blowing out a breath, I stare up at the ceiling. "Can we just take this one major life event at a time? I mean, it's bad enough Mads showed up unannounced while Isaac and I were naked in bed."

Vienna doubles over in laughter. "No, he didn't," she wheezes even as I nod solemnly.

"He did. And Isaac refused to hide in the closet—just in case—so I had to throw a robe on and convince Mads—after he had a snack—to get the hell out." Vienna laughs harder, and I can't help but chuckle at the memory.

"That is priceless."

"He kept asking why I looked so flushed and told me I should sit down."

"And you didn't tell him then?"

"Of course I didn't tell him then." I gasp with not so feigned horror. "Hey Mads, know how you told Isaac and me that we could only be together once and when we broke up you reminded us then and every day since that we *promised* we'd never do this again? Well, we lied and we're having sex—when you got here, in fact—and we're still totally in love even if we haven't said it but you're cool with that, right?"

"I don't see anything wrong with that."

"Are you honestly saying that your brother would be cool about you dating his best friend?"

"Well, Montana's best friend is a girl he is in love with, so I think there'd be a mess all around." I open my mouth to speak but close it just as quick. Vienna notices and puts her hand over mine. "Have you ever just talked to Maddox about it? Like as adults? You and Isaac clearly still love each other. Wouldn't he want you both to be happy?"

"Honestly, I have no idea. I just... I don't know. I was so angry when I left and..." I take a breath and voice my biggest fear and my biggest reason for staying away. "Can Mads and I both survive here? Can we both live in Love Beach without me losing myself again? I've worked too hard over the years to just let all that progress wash away with the tide."

"That ending was a little dramatic," she says with a little smirk.

"Yeah? Well, just wait until my twin actually does find out something is going on with his best friend."

"It will only get worse the longer you wait."

Blowing out a breath, I nod and concede. "Let's just get

through my meeting with Mr. Gomes and then we can tackle my brother disowning me."

"Dramatic," Vienna hisses and I roll my eyes.

"Yeah, well, I can say with certainty I got it from my mother."

16

REECE

The clock on the bedside table moves agonizingly slow, the number seemingly at a standstill as I check and recheck my outfit for tomorrow. My phone vibrates from somewhere on the bed, and I have to hunt through the discarded clothing items to find it.

Snatching it up from under a pencil skirt, I gasp as I read and reread the message.

MADDOX: There was a fire at Cakeology

REECE: WHAT?! I'm on my way!

MADDOX: NO

REECE: What the hell do you mean NO? Is Marigold okay?!

MADDOX: Smoke inhalation but she's okay—refused to go to the hospital

REECE: But she's okay? I can't believe you didn't make her go

MADDOX: Believe me I tried

MADDOX: But I need you to do something for me

REECE: Anything

MADDOX: I have more to do at the shop but I fucked up with Marigold—with how I handled it

REECE: Shocker (eyeroll emoji)

MADDOX: Yell at me later

REECE: Sorry—it's so rare you admit you're in the wrong

MADDOX: Can you focus?

MADDOX: Her shop is a mess and is going to take heavy renovations to get it back up and running.

REECE: That's so awful—what can I do? Is she at her apartment? I can go now.

MADDOX: Logan is with her—the guy who works there

REECE: I love Logan! He's hilarious

MADDOX: FOCUS

Summer with a Brother's Best Friend 73

REECE: I'm multitasking. I'm texting him now for an update

MADDOX: Fine. Whatever. Just go over tomorrow and make sure she's okay. I put a call in to the Probie's parents—they're going to let her use their place to do her baking—we'll take care of the cleanup here. Probie is bringing the dumpster in the morning

REECE: Jace is the Probie, right?

MADDOX: Does it matter? Yes. Just tell Marigold it's all taken care of.

REECE: You DO have a sweet side! She's going to be so happy you did that.

MADDOX: You have to tell her it was you.

REECE: What? Why?

MADDOX: Because. I. Fucked. Up.

REECE: Well, don't wait too long to un-fuck up

MADDOX: Thanks for the advice

REECE: I'm serious. She's amazing and so are you. You deserve amazing.

MADDOX: I gotta go

Figures. Just when I'm trying to get it through his thick skull. I'm about to type back a snarky response when three little bubbles appear and then disappear before a message pops up.

> MADDOX: Love you, Sissy.
>
> REECE: Love you even when I don't like you for hurting Marigold
>
> MADDOX: I'll fix it

Sighing, I throw my phone onto the bed beside me. Isaac is closing the bar tonight with Vienna while I was supposed to be preparing for my meeting with Mr. Gomes. I was supposed to get my thoughts in order and make a plan.

Instead, I had nothing but time to think about Isaac and wonder if I could honestly walk away again. Tension with my brother—and my parents—all seems so trivial after news of the fire.

I just want to see my friend with my own two eyes and make sure she's okay. I want to help her rebuild her dream. And I want us both to get our happily ever afters.

Setting an alarm so I can grab coffees before I see Marigold, I text Isaac a quick update before turning off the light. With any luck, everything will be clearer in the morning.

ISAAC

"Seriously, what is the matter with you?" Vienna asks as we stack the chairs onto the tables.

"You're going to have to be more specific," I say as the exhaustion sets in following messages from Maddox and a couple from Reece. Honestly, it was hard not to close the bar down and race over there once we heard the sirens.

But Maddox would have been pissed at the distraction and not so subtly reminded me I know better.

"You're just going to let Reece leave. After everything y'all have been through, sneaking around and being all *in love*," she says pointedly.

"It's not that easy and—"

"Oh for fuck's sake, you moron—yes it is. She's the happiest I've ever seen her, and you have done nothing but fall all over yourself being the best damn unofficial boyfriend the South has ever seen."

"You really know how to build a man up," I say wryly. Vienna rolls her eyes with a huff.

"Are you just going to let her go? Are you not going to fight for her?"

"I can't make her stay, Vienna," I say a little louder than I intended, but she just squares off with me, hands on her hips and a glare that would make most men cower in fear.

Too bad I'm not one of them.

"Did you ask her?" I press my lips into a firm line and she scoffs. "Or maybe you'd consider moving with her?"

"This bar is—"

"Not keeping you warm at night." I open my mouth to

retort, but she doesn't give me the chance. "It's also not giving you babies, or walking down the aisle to you, or sucking your cock so expertly that your girlfriend's roommate has to wear earplugs to bed when you're over."

My cheeks heat, but I can't deny anything she just said.

Also am I really that loud? I mean, Reece totally is...

Vienna snaps her fingers in front of my face, jolting me back to the present.

"I have never seen two people so completely oblivious about what's in front of them. You love her, Nowak; don't let her go." She picks up a chair and pushes it into my arms. "And if you do, maybe you should think about going with her."

We stare at each other for a minute before I nod. "I'll figure it out."

"Good. I'm going home so I can prepare for whatever shitstorm y'all stir up."

"You really have a way with words, you know that?"

"It's my superpower, and we're either going to need champagne or tequila after tomorrow."

"What about you?"

"What about me? I'm enjoying my fling and saying goodbye when it's over. It's what I want, and I'm happy with it being temporary, but what I have? It's not what you have. Stop trying to make it be more complicated than it is. You love her, Isaac. Show her what that means."

It's not until Vienna is gone that I realize I'm still holding the chair. Mind racing, I place it on the ground and drop into it like the weight of the world is resting on my shoulders and look around.

All I've ever wanted was to run this bar—to bring joy to tourists and locals alike—and to keep the things I love most about Love Beach front and center both as a businessman and neighbor.

And I've done that.

But it's never come close to how I feel when I'm with Reece. Vienna was right, about more than I'd like to admit, and I know what I have to do.

17

REECE

"Reece! Please, come in!" Mr. Gomes says cheerfully, his eyes crinkling at the corners like he's truly happy to see me. He offers me his hand, and we shake as if I haven't hugged this man a million times at various gatherings around town.

"Thank you so much for seeing me," I reply, taking the seat across from him.

"Of course. I'm sorry we haven't been able to connect before now." His tone is sincere, and we talk about his trip and some of the more mundane things happening in Love Beach before he pulls a manila folder from the center drawer and places it on the desk in front of him.

"I'd really like to know why you think I'd be a good fit here," I ask, and his returning smile is knowing as he pushes the folder toward me.

"I had a feeling after the last time we spoke that you were under the impression this position was a favor to your family." I hold his gaze but remain silent. The words are uncomfortable, but I appreciate him giving them life—because he's right, I have wondered about that.

A lot.

Mr. Gomes nods toward the folder, and with thankfully steady hands, I lift it from the desk and flip it open. Dozens of articles with my name stare back at me for events I helped put on, awards I'd received, and thanks from the school and community.

"Each candidate had a folder like that—things that went beyond just showing up for their job. Your folder is remarkably bigger than the rest." My cheeks heat as he continues, "Your family has always been a pillar in our community but that"—he points at the stack of papers—"is what you've managed to accomplish out in the world all on your own."

"I don't know what to say," I admit, thumbing through the pages and smiling at the memories of moments past.

"Your father, and especially your brother, have taken every opportunity to tell me how impressive your teaching career has been. And I have to agree." He nods again at the folder in my hands. "Your enthusiasm and heart precede you, Reece. Teaching at any level requires a certain disposition, and I'd argue that's especially true for wrangling high school students."

"They're certainly a challenge."

"A challenge you've met head-on and exceeded the expectations put forth. I didn't offer you the job because your father and I have a standing golf date or because your brother always makes sure he's available for demonstrations or assemblies in the district."

I blow out a breath and stare out the window over his shoulder as I let his words sink in. This is what I've wanted.

What I've *always* wanted—to be seen and valued for what I bring to the table. And now that I'm here, it's more difficult to accept than I imagined.

"You can have more time if you need to think about it,"

Mr. Gomes says carefully as if he's worried I might bolt at any second. But I shake my head because he's wrong.

"I'd very much like to accept the position."

Mr. Gomes's smile is immediate as it stretches across his face, and I can't help but do the same as I feel the invisible weight lift from my shoulders. The last thing I ever wanted to do was end up back in Love Beach with a million "I told you sos" and disapproving stares.

But I guess I also forgot all the magic I'd found here too. I'd missed the sand and the ocean and being wrapped up in Isaac's arms every night.

I missed him.

And honestly, I could go anywhere for a job, but I want a life too, and the only one I want to live it with is Isaac.

"You had me sweatin' bullets, and I was born and raised in South Carolina, Miss Baylor." He winks and I chuckle as he stands. "Let's show you to your classroom and then we can swing back here and grab your paperwork."

"That sounds perfect."

18

REECE

I'm practically vibrating with excitement as I park in front of Love Beach Brews and climb out. Today has been surreal, and I can't wait to tell Isaac my news. Climbing out, I stop short when I see he's talking to a woman just inside. Her long, black ponytail swings back and forth as she nods along to something he said.

His posture is *tense,* and he rubs the back of his neck with his hand before nodding a final time and watching her turn and leave. She doesn't see me as she pushes out the door and walks straight to her car, phone in hand.

I don't like it.

And I like it less when I burst into the bar, startling Isaac who had still been staring at the woman with the raven hair.

"Who the hell was that, Isaac?"

His gaze snaps to me and he swallows hard. "Saige."

"Saige Reiser?"

"Yeah," he says, somehow defeated and also resolved.

"What was she doing here?"

"She's a real estate agent."

"You buying something?" I ask with my hands on my

hips, suddenly defensive as the adrenaline rush from earlier takes a nose dive.

"Possibly. But probably selling."

"Selling what?" I ask, dropping my hands as I follow his gaze around the bar.

Isaac takes a breath and then reaches for me, pulling me against him. "Saige is going to look at places out by you in North Carolina and see if there's an opportunity for me to open another location while keeping this one up and running, but I may need to sell."

"What?" I gasp, rearing back to look him in the eyes. "But you love this place and Jimmy Buffet and Love Beach and that wine from the Book & Barrel and—"

"And none of that matters if I'm not with you, Reece. The last seven years have felt like an eternity and then you came home and it's been everything I could ever dream of, and so nothing else matters. Not the bar or this town or your brother. I gave you up for him once. I won't do it again."

Tears prick the back of my eyes as I push up onto tiptoes to wrap my arms around his neck. "But you don't have to."

"Reece, I'm not kidding. I'll—"

I slant my mouth over his, stealing the words from his lips with a hard kiss. Isaac groans and holds me tighter, misunderstanding my enthusiasm and forcing me to chuckle as I pull away.

"You don't have to choose because I'm home. I'm staying."

Eyes wide, he gapes at me. "What?"

"I went and talked to Mr. Gomes today and formally accepted the job. He was impressed with *me*. My contributions to the school and the programs I've been involved with."

"Of course he was impressed with you; you're fucking

amazing," he says before peppering my face with kisses and making me giggle and squirm against him.

"Oh my gosh, you're ridiculous." I laugh as he nuzzles against my neck, his beard tickling the sensitive skin.

"But you're staying?"

"Yes," I say with a confidence that radiates from every cell in my body. "I want to build a life with you here." Huffing, I add, "If I wasn't so stubborn, I could have saved us all a lot of time and heartache."

Isaac brushes his thumb over my cheek, his palm cradling my face. "I think it had to be this way." He gives me a sad smile. "You needed to grow up away from all this, and even though it fucking killed me to let you go in college, I know you would've resented me if you'd come back when we graduated."

I don't disagree with him because I can't. I'd needed space, and I hadn't gotten that with Maddox still involved in every waking moment of my life.

"Do you think he'll be mad?"

Isaac shrugs, but I can see the worry marring his handsome face. "We'll deal with it. I was willing to sell my bar and move out of Love Beach to be with you." His lips twist up in a crooked grin. "Nothing he can do about me finally making you my wife."

"You better not be proposing to me in your bar," I say, half teasing but mostly serious.

Isaac's hands slide down my body to grip my ass, picking me up and forcing me to wrap my legs around his waist as he walks us into the storage room, kicking the door closed behind us.

"Are you saying you wouldn't marry me if I asked you right now?" The door is cold against my back as he presses me against it, his lips hovering a breath away from mine.

"You know I'd say yes, but you better not be asking me right now."

"I'm not asking you, Reece, but I *will* be asking you real soon; you can count on that."

"Better tell Saige you won't be selling or buying anytime soon."

"Dunno, Baby, maybe we should start looking for houses."

I sigh as he kisses up the column of my neck, my fingers gripping and tugging at his hair as I arch into his touch.

"We need to wait until after we tell Mads."

"Let's go right now," he murmurs against my skin, his tongue dipping into the valley between my breasts as he pulls the front of my dress down. Isaac sucks my nipple into his mouth, and I hold him tighter against me as a shiver races down my spine.

"We have to wait until after the party." The last word is a moan as his hand slides up my thigh and under the hem of my dress. "We just need to get through that then—"

I gasp as the rough pad of his finger slides between my folds and then circles my clit with the exact pressure and speed to get me off.

"Not a second longer," he growls, my orgasm ricocheting through me as the promise of his words washes over me.

19

REECE

Only a few more hours and then I'm free.
I repeat the words like I can somehow will this party to go smoothly and to my mother's standards even though she claimed the details didn't matter.

They did.

Good Lord, did they matter.

"Hey Ba... Reece," Isaac catches himself as my eyes flare wide, "where do you want these flowers?"

"Those go over on the gift table," I say, pointing across the room as I will my heart rate to slow. We're too close to the end of keeping our relationship a secret to blow it now, but I'm craving his touch more than ever.

Especially today.

I'm so focused on sorting the favors I don't hear Maddox come in behind me.

"Hey, Reece."

"Hey, Brother," I say, immediately defensive even though I don't want to be. "Can you go get the balloons from my car?"

He doesn't answer, lingering in the room before huffing

and spinning on his heels. I don't have time for this today, but more than that, I hate that we've been practically strangers since I've been back.

"Baby, are you okay?" Isaac asks, wrapping his arms around me and letting me bury my face in his chest. We shouldn't be doing this, but I can't deny how badly I need his strength right now.

"I'm so tired," I admit, listening for footsteps outside the room and hearing none.

"Well, I did keep you up late," Isaac murmurs, tilting my chin up with his finger to lick along the seam of my lips, forcing a giggle from me before fully pressing his mouth to mine. *This* is what I needed, and—

"What the fuck is this?!" Maddox's voice booms through the space, making me jump as I turn to face him.

Hours pass in the span of seconds as I watch a myriad of emotions flit across my brother's face.

"I'm not doing this today," he barks, stomping down the hall back toward the parking lot.

"No!" I growl, chasing after him, with Isaac right behind me. "Mads, you're going to listen to me. This has gone on long enough!"

"Not today, Sissy."

"Dammit, Mads!" My heels click against the pavement as he finally stops to face me.

"You're together now, aren't you? You couldn't even tell me? You're doing exactly what I asked you not to do!"

"Yeah, we're together and we're happy, and I need you to be happy for us!"

"I get that you wanted more than Love Beach, but why couldn't you just stay? Why did it take you so long to come back?"

"I *am* staying! If you would've pulled your head out of your ass for five seconds, I would have been able to tell you that. But you're too busy spending every waking moment obsessed with your job instead of putting that time into building a relationship with the first girl who's ever been able to tolerate you!" My words are loud and hurtful, but I can't stop them, and even though I should want to take them back, I don't. He needs to hear them as much as I needed to say them.

Car doors slam, and belatedly, I know it's Marigold and someone else, but I can't take my eyes off Maddox. He's angry and hurt and so am I. He was right. We shouldn't be doing this here, but we're like a freight train running off the tracks.

"It's not about leaving you, Mads. I needed space, and I needed to be somewhere where I was just *me*, where I could avoid disappointing our parents for not going into nursing, where I wasn't just your sister."

"But you couldn't tell me? You couldn't tell me any of that, so you just broke his heart right along with mine?"

Logan materializes next to me, nodding toward the cake in his hands. The cake for my parents.

For their anniversary party.

Shit.

"Ladies, come help me take this inside," he says to me and Marigold, and I follow because it's too much, and I need a minute to breathe.

But there's no time for that because as soon as the cake is on the table, Logan spins on both of us.

"Talk," he says pointedly at me.

"I almost murdered my brother, but I can't because he loves you," I admit with a huff as I look at Marigold.

"Pretty sure I would've helped you bury his body."

Logan motions at his clothes. "These are not 'let's commit felonies' clothes."

"And he hasn't said he loves me."

I snort and then turn and take Marigold's hand. "Take it from the girl who suppressed her feelings for her brother's best friend and then was sneaking around with him all summer." We exchange a grin before sobering. "I want you to be happy, and if my brother is the one who does that,"—I swallow hard—"you need to fight for him. He's not always easy to love, but he's a good man."

"And hot," Logan says and we chuckle. "Ready?" I know he's not just asking her, but I *am* ready. I'm ready to rebuild my relationship with my brother, I'm ready to start my life with Isaac, and I'm ready to finally let myself be happy in Love Beach.

Nodding, we follow the path back out into the parking lot where Isaac and Maddox are still engaged in a heated conversation.

But it's not about us—it's about him and Marigold, and my heart swells as my brother finally realizes his girl is behind him.

It's the rawest moment I've ever witnessed—Maddox pouring his heart out and giving in to his own happily ever after.

My smile grows as I wrap myself around Isaac and smirk. "Do you get it now, Maddox?" Waving between our respective partners, I add, "She's my friend, he's yours; pretty easy to blur that line."

We laugh and talk about what's to come—what we can look forward to. I tell him more about my job at the high school and my struggle with our mother's constant criticism. Maddox seems surprised by the latter, but now's not the time to do a deep dive on twenty plus years of failed expectations.

"I needed something more than just being your sister, and I needed to follow my dreams. Nursing school was never part of that."

My brother nods, taking it all in, and I'm thankful to finally share my feelings with him.

It's only belatedly that I realize my parents have arrived, my mother taking the opportunity to remind us that the party will be starting soon.

And are you sure everything is ready?

I nod, my father offering encouraging words for my mother and us. But my mother has never left well enough alone, and like she can't help herself, she has to have the last word. Specifically, how she can't believe I'm still complaining about nursing not being my calling and *we know your little teaching job is important to you.*

Isaac's hand reaches for mine as Logan pops up to usher everyone into the hall.

It's a blessing and a curse we were interrupted, because I don't have the energy to fight with her today.

So while we follow everyone inside, I repeat the mantra I started the day with.

Only a few more hours and then I'm free.

20

ISAAC

"Baby, you need to relax," I murmur to Reece, pressing a kiss to the top of her head as I draw little circles on the small of her back.

"Coat closet." Vienna coughs dramatically and I can't even roll my eyes because it gets Reece to crack a smile.

"I wish," Reece says dreamily, like being partially naked surrounded by cleaning supplies would be better than this. Honestly, she's probably right.

Today has been exhausting, and most of it hasn't even been about me. The standoff with Maddox in the parking lot had been a shit show and not how I wanted him to find out about me and his sister.

But it was also cathartic too.

For all of us.

We'd all made mistakes, but they didn't have to define where we went from here.

"It will be over soon, I promise," I say, pulling my girl against me, and *God* does it feel good not to have to hide.

"Maddox looks happy," she says, her gaze following him and Marigold as they walk around the room.

"He should be—got his girl and his sister back all in the same parking lot."

"I'm so sorry I missed that," Vienna muses.

"You got the highlights," Reece says with a shrug.

"Completely unrelated…"—I pause looking between the two of them—"I forgot that I put an ad out for a brewmaster; everything happened so fast over this past week, but I got a reply yesterday."

"That's great. Do you think they'll interview?" Reece asks and I nod.

"I spoke to him on the phone, just a casual conversation, but he said that he'd be moving and would need help caring for his daughter and asked if I had anyone who might be interested if he got the job." I stare at the side of Vienna's head until she turns toward me.

"What are you looking at me like that for?"

"I dunno. I just thought you might be interested in nannying?"

"Trying to boot me from the bar, Nowak?"

"Of course not," I say as Reece snickers. "I just thought you could use a little extra to help get your flower shop up and running."

Her eyes snap to Reece. "You told him?"

"Because I was so excited about us both being here and staying. It's an incredible idea, and you're going to be amazing, and I just couldn't keep it to myself."

Vienna's gaze softens as she wraps Reece in a hug. "I don't deserve you sometimes."

"You deserve all the things."

"Hello, everyone," Reece's father says into the microphone, his wife by his side. Their relationship was one I'd never get used to. Bill always seemed too nice to be with

Candee, but I guess stranger things have happened considering this party is to celebrate a marriage milestone.

Bill goes through the general thank yous before Candee asks Reece and Maddox to join them on stage. I can tell that Reece would rather get a root canal than go up there by the way her shoulders stiffen.

I could almost kiss Maddox when he walks over and offers her his hand, walking up together.

A united front.

Thankfully.

Because when Candee makes another passive-aggressive comment about Reece being a teacher in Love Beach, it's Maddox who takes the mic.

And it's all I can do to stay rooted in my spot.

My best friend goes on about how he's always wanted to follow in his father's footsteps—it's a story I know by heart—but that's not what has a lump forming in my throat.

No, it's the way that in front of this crowded room, Maddox finally gives Reece the love and acknowledgment she deserves. He talks about how Love Beach High School sought out Reece to teach there, about how proud he is of her.

But most importantly, it's directed at Candee. It's something she can't ignore, and I hope she doesn't.

She seems...moved—like maybe she truly couldn't see the harm her words had done to her daughter.

"Fucking finally," Vienna mutters next to me, my head whipping to her as I catch Candee hugging Reece out of the corner of my eye.

"What?" I laugh.

"He finally pulled his head out of his ass and stood up to their mom." She shakes her head. "My brother is a lot of things, but hell hath no fury like Montana Greene when someone messes with his family."

"That's amazing."

"What's amazing is that you're in love with a girl who looks like your best friend." Vienna smirks and I bark out a laugh.

"Ouch."

"I've been dying to use that one, and it's taken forever for the right moment."

"Well, I'm glad, because this will be a moment I cherish for the rest of my days," I deadpan, and she does a dramatic hair flip that has me shaking my head.

"As you should."

"Just you wait, Vienna. Some guy is gonna sweep you off your feet, and you'll be just as dopey as the rest of us in love."

She wrinkles her nose and scoffs. "Why would you say such horrible things to me?"

"What are y'all talking about?" Reece asks, coming over and wrapping her arm around my waist as she sags against my body.

"Just telling Vienna I can't wait for her to fall in love and live happily ever after."

Reece snorts and Vienna rolls her eyes. "You can *keep* your happily ever after. I'm perfectly *happy* with just right now."

I open my mouth to speak when Logan's voice rises above the rest.

"Can I have everyone's attention? It's time to cut the cake!"

21

REECE

"I'm proud of you," Isaac whispers into my hair as we walk along the sand, our fingers intertwined, the breeze a gentle caress after a long day.

"Thank you for being here with me."

Isaac pulls me to a stop and brushes a lock of hair behind my ear. "There's nowhere else I want to be."

His lips are soft but firm against mine, a kiss to seal a promise, rather than the fiery passion we've become accustomed to.

We'd lived a lifetime in the span of a few hours today. Maddox had defended me in a crowded room, and I'd never been more terrified or thankful for my brother than in that moment.

Our mother had been surprisingly shocked by what he said, and we'd had a moment on the stage where it felt like everything might be okay. She'd hugged me tight again before we left and promised that she'd do better—make up for the way she'd pushed her own aspirations on me instead of building me up like I deserved.

But I didn't need all of that. I just wanted a clean slate so we could enjoy the present and future instead of dwelling in the past. We already had a tentative date to play tennis next week to catch up, and then she surprised the hell out of me when she offered to help set up my classroom for the fall.

Maddox had snickered at that, and she'd volunteered him for all the heavy lifting.

I wasn't mad about it.

We all healed a little today, forgiving the things we couldn't change and making promises for all the things we had to look forward to.

"Mr. Nowak, it's not dark enough out here for your wandering hands," I murmur against his lips as he grips my ass through the cotton fabric of my dress.

"Can't be helped, and besides,"—he pulls me tight against his body, his erection digging into my belly—"I thought you liked the thrill of people watching."

"Almost watching. I like the idea that we *could* get caught —not actually getting caught."

He chuckles and pulls away, taking my hand again as we head toward the car.

"Well, let's get you home so I can get you out of that dress and coming all over my face."

"I love everything about that sentence," I purr. And I do. I love that he worships my body like a starving man, and I love the idea that after all this time, we finally get to be *home*.

"Good. We'll get you moved in tomorrow, and you can act like your shoes don't take up half my closet space already."

"Act like you don't like it."

"I'm already imagining you strutting around the house naked in every pair of heels."

"That's wildly impractical."

"Not in my mind it's not."

I snort as we make our way onto the sidewalk, the streetlights blinking on as Love Beach's nightlife awakens. Signs glow and fairy lights twinkle in the distance, and I can't help the sigh that escapes because there really is no place like this town.

Like home.

"What's that look for?" Isaac asks, pausing by the passenger side door.

"I'm just happy. I'm relieved and exhausted in the best possible way and praying we don't have to deal with any other theatrics from our family and friends."

"And?" he asks with a smile tugging at the corner of his mouth.

"And I'm happy to be here with you and cannot wait to be your wife."

Isaac presses me against the side of the car, boxing me in with his body and threading his fingers in my hair. "I'm going to take every opportunity to call you *my wife* just like in those books you read."

His face nuzzles into the crook of my neck, and I gasp as he peppers kisses along my jaw. "I just don't want a big wedding."

"Three days ago you told me I couldn't propose yet," Isaac croons against the shell of my ear.

"And three days ago you told me it would happen *real soon.*"

"We can have whatever kind of wedding you want, but I need to get you home."

"Courthouse?"

"Maybe not," he says, finally looking up at me.

I pout and he chuckles, shaking his head as he says,

"You'd be sad not having your brother and Marigold, Vienna, and your parents there."

"I feel like we've already shared so much of our relationship with other people, and I just want something for *us*."

"Okay, how about this,"—his thumb trails over my bottom lip—"intimate ceremony, extended honeymoon, and then a casual reception when we get home."

I open my mouth to speak and then tilt my head to the side as the idea takes hold. "We'll have to honeymoon over Christmas break."

Isaac nods. "Vienna and the new guy, if I hire him, will be able to watch the bar while we're gone. I can find extra coverage if we need it."

"I don't want to wait that long to get married though."

"Well, Ms. Baylor," he says with a wicked grin, "how do you feel about the end of summer?"

"I think we better start planning, Mr. Nowak."

"I've been planning all day, Baby."

I look at him in surprise. "You have?"

"Yeah, I've been planning on how to get you out of that dress since you put it on."

He laughs and I roll my eyes. "You're such a romantic," I muse as he holds my door open for me.

"I'll do it right; don't you worry."

"I'm not worried," I say, grabbing his shirt and pulling him down for a kiss. "All I need is you."

"And most of the closet and dresser space. And another bookshelf and—"

"Get in the car, Nowak. You owe your future wife some orgasms."

Isaac laughs, walking around the hood of the car before dropping into the driver's seat. Without a word, he cups my face and slants his mouth over mine in a searing kiss before resting his forehead against mine.

"Best summer ever," he says quietly.

"Best summer ever."

With my brother's best friend.

EPILOGUE
ISAAC

THE LAST DAY OF SUMMER

"Do you think they suspect anything?" Reece asks as we line up the beach chairs under the tent. Her white sundress is covering the white bikini underneath, the one she bought especially for today. Her hair is pulled up into a ponytail, with little wisps falling around her makeup-free face—because this is how she wanted to marry me.

And I absolutely love it.

I can't stop the grin that stretches over my face as I stare at her. "Pretty sure they'll suspect something as soon as they get here."

Coolers with chilled champagne and an assortment of easy-to-eat beach foods sit off to the side, a smaller one holding beautiful flower leis, all made by Vienna.

She'd agreed to officiate our impromptu ceremony and had been appalled when we'd told her we weren't doing any of the traditional things—like flowers. She wouldn't take no for an answer which is how we ended up with the floral-filled cooler.

"Hey y'all," Vienna says, hustling across the sand, "they're here!"

I expect Reece to look nervous, but she just flashes me the biggest smile as Maddox and Marigold come into view.

"Oh my God!" Marigold screeches, tossing her sand chair down before wrapping Reece in a crushing hug. She squeals again and does a little dance, and I can only assume she's just agreed to be Reece's maid of honor.

"What is..." Maddox starts before pushing his sunglasses up on the top of his head.

"Be my best man?"

"No fucking way, dude," he says with a laugh and then wraps me in a hug and slaps my back. "I'd be honored."

Vienna places a purple and white flower lei around Marigold's neck before doing the same to Maddox, their cheesy grins a welcome reprieve as I spot Reece's parents.

I brace for the worst as Bill and Candee stop short of the tent, their eyes taking everything in as Candee's hand goes to her mouth.

I'd asked Bill's permission, but Lord knows they weren't expecting it to happen so quickly. My own parents had been disappointed but understanding when we'd called them earlier this week, their cross-country trip already in progress and making it impossible to get home in time.

But this was only the beginning. They'd be back for the reception and every milestone after.

"Mr. Baylor," Vienna says, slipping the flower lei over Bill's head.

"I was hoping you'd *both* walk me down the aisle," Reece says quietly, her mother wiping frantically at the tears rolling down her cheeks as she nods.

"Of course! Oh my goodness, Bill, how is my hair?"

"You look great, Mom," Reece says, her eyes shiny as Vienna places a stunning flower lei around Candee's neck.

"Everyone ready?" Vienna asks, and I nod, following her to the front of the tent, where she places an all-white lei around my neck before yelling, "Pretend there's music!"

Everyone chuckles, and I feel myself relax as I watch Marigold and Maddox walking arm in arm toward me. They break apart, Maddox moving to stand behind me while Marigold moves to stand across from me, leaving space for my bride.

My breath hitches in my throat as my bride links her arms with her parents and takes her first step toward me—toward our future.

Her eyes well with unshed tears, and I have to blink like hell to keep mine at bay. I've almost made it when Maddox's hand lands on my shoulder, and I have to choke back a sob because I never thought we'd get here.

I never thought I'd be marrying Reece—never thought I'd have Maddox's blessing and definitely never dreamed we'd be able to do this in Love Beach.

But this is perfect—it's everything I've ever wanted.

Everything I dreamed of.

Because it's her.

Reece kisses her father on the cheek and then turns and wraps her mother in a hug. They stand like that for a long moment before Bill takes Candee's hand, and Reece places her hands in mine.

"And for the most perfect bride," Vienna says quietly, placing an all-white lei around Reece's neck to match my own. "I'm so happy for you."

"I love you," Reece whispers, and Vienna gives a watery smile before clearing her throat.

"Dearly beloved, we are gathered here today to celebrate the love and commitment of two of my very favorite people..."

THE END

Read about Vienna and her mystery man in Merry with a Brewmaster coming Fall 2024.

Read Next in the Love Beach collection: Summer with a Fireman and Summer with a Player!

Be sure to check out the rest of the books in the Multi-Author Love Beach Collection.

Also, the Love Beach Authors invite you to join us for more fun including free Ebooks, giveaways, cocktail recipes, and more on the Love Beach Fan Page.

ACKNOWLEDGMENTS

I'd like to start by saying thank you to my husband for keeping me grounded through this journey. We'll always be better together.

To my family for their complete and unwavering support and enthusiasm. I couldn't ask for a better cheering section.

To Atlee for holding me accountable even when I didn't want you to – you're a rockstar and I'm so thankful to have you in my corner. To Lindsey, thank you for pushing me to be better and being the good cop to Atlee's bad cop – you girls are the best!

To Nicole for loving my lasagna recipe and the forever friendship we've forged. I'm so thankful we get to walk this path together. To my Books, Babes & Bombshells I love you so big!

To Carolina for making me jump on this wild ride - thank you. This was so much fun to write with you and I cannot wait for all that's to come!

To J. Hutchison thank you for all the writing sprints and keeping me going even when I didn't want to. You are the amazing!

To AK Cover Designs for jumping in and creating the paperback for me!

To my author and book friends turned real friends and the writing community (there are so many of you!) – your support has been overwhelming and I am truly humbled. Thank you for being on this journey with me.

To my ARC/Street Team – I still can't believe I have one of those – thank you. You showed up and went above and beyond for me, y'all are the best!

To the readers who took a chance on me – thank you. I'll never be able to say it enough. You've already exceeded my wildest dreams.

To the Anns of Happily Editing Anns – you're the real unsung heroes of this adventure. Thank you for walking me through hours and hours of editing – those side margin notes are gold. To Gina who nurtured my passion for writing – thank you for seeing my potential – I hope I always make you proud.

To my cheering squad who never let a day go by without kind words of encouragement or that swift kick to get me going – you're the absolute best! You know who you are and I love you more than words.

ABOUT THE AUTHOR

Alexandra Hale is a small town girl living with her family in Upstate New York. She routinely runs on caffeine, dry shampoo and thrives on procrastination.

A lover of all things romance, Alexandra finally began putting pen to paper shortly after graduating college. An unobtainable dream has slowly become a reality with the love and support of her friends and family and the romance community.

She currently writes steamy, small town romance with a dash of lighthearted fun and happily ever afters that will make you swoon.

Connect with Alexandra here!

ALSO BY ALEXANDRA HALE

Blackstone Falls

Secretly Falling (A Blackstone Novella)

Feels Like Falling (Blackstone Falls Book 1)

Unexpectedly Falling (Preorder Summer 2024)

Clementine Creek

Back in the Country

Making it Country

Home in the Country

Out in the Country (A Standalone Novella)

Playing it Country

Christmas in Kiwi Country (A Clementine Creek Novella 4.5)

Forever in the Country

Loving it Country (A Newsletter Freebie)

Love Beach

Summer with a Brother's Best Friend

Merry with a Brewmaster (Fall 2024)

Magnolia Point (Man of the Month)

Watermelon With You? (August 2024)

Ironwood (TBD)

Staged (An Ironwood Crossing Novel, Book 1)

Made in the USA
Middletown, DE
28 July 2024

58049355R00071